HARLEY HITCH
AND THE FOSSIL MYSTERY

HARLEY HITCH

AND THE FOSSIL MYSTERY

VASHTI HARDY

ILLUSTRATED BY
GEORGE ERMOS

◢SCHOLASTIC

Published in the UK by Scholastic, 2023
1 London Bridge, London, SE1 9BG
Scholastic Ireland, 89E Lagan Road,
Dublin Industrial Estate, Glasnevin, Dublin, D11 HP5F

ISBN 978 0702 32343 0

A CIP catalogue record for this book
is available from the British Library.

Printed by CPI Group (UK) Ltd, Croydon, CR0 4YY
Paper made from wood grown in sustainable forests
and other controlled sources.

1 3 5 7 9 10 8 6 4 2

www.scholastic.co.uk

For Jude and Mabel

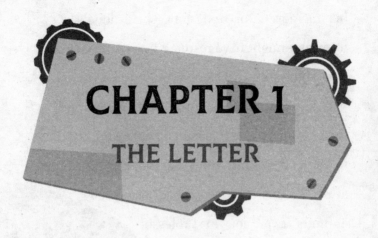

CHAPTER 1
THE LETTER

A letter arrived the week before the school summer term was due to start. It was addressed to *Harley Hitch, care of Grandpas Elliot and Eden, Hitch House, Forgetown*. Harley recognized the silver cog stamp of her school in the corner of the envelope.

Sprocket, Harley's robot pet, tilted his head and gave an inquisitive *yip!*

What could it be about? Holding the letter as

though it might detonate, Harley searched her memories for something she'd done last term that might have resulted in a suspension. She'd had a few disasters, of course. The moon had disappeared, which was pretty major news in Forgetown, but that had all turned out well in the end, and it hadn't been because of her after all. But then there had also been a minor explosion in Professor Horatio's lesson when she'd been creative with the composting formula in the Cogworks greenhouse…

"What have you got there?" Grandpa Elliot asked, as he breezed into the hallway of Hitch House, buttoning his waistcoat.

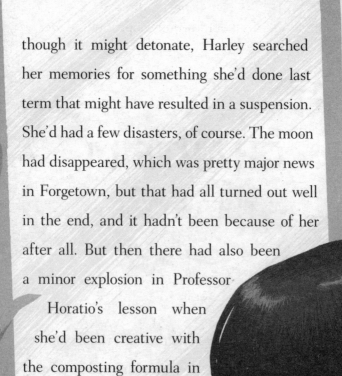

Harley swiftly put the envelope behind her back. "Nothing."

Grandpa Elliot raised an eyebrow. "That looked like a Cogworks' stamp to me! Come, now, Harley, it must be important." He put his hands on his hips.

Harley sighed and reluctantly opened the letter. She read it quickly, then breathed out in relief. "I'm not suspended! It's from Professor Spark. She says there's a new teacher, Professor Anning, who is running a school trip for our year group at the very start of term. We get to stay away for two whole nights! Woo-hoo!" Harley punched the air excitedly.

"Professor Anning, the esteemed paleontologist?" Grandpa Elliot sounded impressed.

"Paleo-what-what?"

"It means fossil expert."

"Oh, right." Harley didn't know much about fossils, apart from Professor Fretshaw, who she sometimes thought could be a mean old fossil.

"What's the whooping about?" Grandpa Eden

walked through the front door holding a red cabbage in one hand and a bit of tree root in the other.

"There's a new professor at Cogworks," said Grandpa Elliot. "Professor Anning!"

"She's a paleo-what-what fossil person, and she's taking us on a school trip!" said Harley, already thinking about what she'd need to pack. How fun it was going to be to have two nights away with her best friend Cosmo and the rest of the class!

"A paleontologist," Grandpa Elliot corrected.

Harley looked back to the letter. "We're going to Inventia Jurassic Coast!"

"How exciting!" said Grandpa Eden.

"Isn't it? The coast! We'll probably be paddling in the sea, building sandcastles, and there'll surely be ice cream…" Harley wondered if she should pack her swimsuit.

"I meant exciting because you'll get to spend

5

time with an extraordinary professor and see some amazing fossils, Harley. Inventia Jurassic Coast is famous for all the fossils that have been found there. You'll have a snapshot of prehistoric history."

"Right, yeah, that too."

"History helps us make sense of the past and understand who we are today. It's important," said Grandpa Elliot.

"But it's not as exciting as seaside chips and ice cream, Grandpa Elliot," Harley teased.

"Oh, I think history is much more exciting. Take this." He pointed to a framed silk square on the wall, which she'd never paid that much attention to. It was navy, red and gold, with an intricate briar pattern on the edge and a lion with a sunburst mane in the middle.

"It belonged to Queen Elizabeth of Inventia from two hundred years ago. Family legend says that the queen was passing through Forgetown on her tour of Inventia. My great-great-great grandfather waited in the rain for so many hours that by the time she arrived he had quite the cold. When the queen passed by, he couldn't contain his sneezing. She paused the whole parade to offer her handkerchief before continuing."

"Wow, really? So we have a royal hanky! Do we have anything else?"

Grandpa Elliot took a small coin from his waistcoat pocket. "This is my lucky coin. My grandma gave it to me. She found it not far from the Iron Forest when she was digging out oil truffles as a girl. She said it was all the way from the Roman times."

Harley could see why being a reporter for the *Forgetown Daily* newspaper suited Grandpa Elliot so much. He loved telling stories.

"Impressive objects," said Grandpa Eden with a smile. "But…" He strode into the living room, and Harley saw him rummage in one of his research draws before returning with a bit of yellowish rock with bits of plant leaves stuck inside. "This is called amber. It's a kind of fossil in which tree sap has fallen into the sea millions of years ago and turned hard, trapping a bit of leaf matter inside it. This is millions of years old!"

"Coooool…" Harley breathed. She wondered what might hang on the walls and inside the draws of Hitch House in the future. Who knew what Forgetown would be like then, and what would be possible? She imagined a rocket ship taking her from her favourite place, the star-chatter observatory, right up to space where she could dance with the stars in the distant sky. Maybe her spacesuit would be mounted like one of the old-fashioned silver suits of armour in castles, for future Hitch family members to admire.

"You both really do love history, don't you?" Harley smiled.

Grandpa Elliot nodded. "One day we'll pass these things on to you. Who knows what you'll find on your trip to start your own collection?"

That did sound kind of cool. "It's going to be the best ever!"

"Then we'd better get you ready," said Grandpa Eden, passing her the red cabbage.

"Er … I don't think I need to pack this." Harley frowned.

He ruffled her hair. "Didn't you want to go purple this term? The cabbage, along with this cherry tree root and a few other things I've been growing should make a vibrant shade."

"Oh, thanks!" Harley loved to dye her hair a different colour each term. It was one of the ways she embraced her individuality.

Her transmitter bleeped in her pocket. She took it out and pressed the button while Grandpa Elliot hurried off to work with a quick hug goodbye, and Grandpa Eden took his plants and vegetables into the kitchen.

"Harley, it's me, Cosmo! Did you get a letter?"

"Yes!"

"Isn't it the most exciting thing?"

"Do you think there'll be dinosaur-sized ice creams?"

"I hope so! And maybe I'll find some fossilized Jurassic plants there!" Cosmo loved plants almost as much as Grandpa Eden, whose garden was the envy of Forgetown.

"I'm going to start packing."

"Me too. I can't wait!" Cosmo said.

"It's going to be epic. See you later, Cosmo."

As she signed off, Sprocket let out a sad whine.

"What's the matter?" Harley crouched down next to him.

Teardrops flashed in his robotic eyes.

"Oh! I forgot to say. According to the letter, we're allowed to bring our robot pets. You're coming too!"

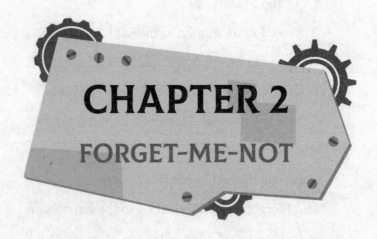

CHAPTER 2
FORGET-ME-NOT

Harley and Sprocket hurried towards Cogworks, Harley's rucksack heavy with extra clothes, which the grandpas had insisted she pack "just in case". It was swelteringly hot, even for this early in the morning, and she had to cover her eyes from the sun being reflected from the distant Iron Forest in eye-aching shards of light.

Harley had rolled up her favourite dungarees

and wore her new red dinosaur-print T-shirt. She'd changed the laces of her big boots to purple to match her hair, and her tool belt jangled at her waist, heavy with all the equipment she thought she might need. Despite the fact she was still mostly looking forward to the seaside treats, Cosmo had insisted they go to the library to research the Jurassic period of Inventia, and she'd taken out a fascinating book on dinosaurs. It was sad they weren't around any more. Grandpa Elliot told her it was all because of an asteroid that hit the planet sixty-six million years ago.

Sprocket bounded happily beside her. With Grandpa Eden's help, they'd made a few adjustments to her robot pet in the past week: they'd added a freezing compartment to make ice cubes, and his tail could now whirl around like a cooling fan.

Just ahead, she gazed at the magnificent twisting steel pipes and tall layered towers of the classroom and laboratory block. The clock on the Cogworks main dome showed that it was almost eight o'clock, an hour earlier than the usual school starting time. And there on the driveway was something that resembled an old-fashioned steam train, with piston wheels and open carriage compartments.

"Whoa, are we going in that?" Harley breathed. A train that didn't need a railway track! She'd heard of the likes in Inventia City, but she had never seen one in Forgetown.

Primbot, the tall, austere gatekeeper robot (who looked remarkably like the head teacher of Cogworks, Professor Fretshaw), stood at the school gate frantically checking off the group of overexcited pupils and their robot pets from a list: Rufus with his budgie bot Awk flying in loops around his head; Lettice and her rabbit Coppertail; Asma and her cat Fluffles; Delores with her snake Marty, and…

Then Harley heard: "Thank goodness I brought sunglasses, because you've obviously set out to blind the lot of us." It was Fenelda Spiggot, who was always ready with a snide dig of some kind. Fenelda's hair had been freshly cut for the new term in her customary blunt bob and fringe, every hair in place, and she wore neatly pressed shorts and a shirt which looked a bit like she was heading off for tea with royalty rather than a school trip to the seaside.

Harley let Fenelda's comment wash over her. She'd long ago learned that any mean words from Fenelda said more about her than Harley.

Fenelda placed a hand on her hip. "Are you going for the forget-me-not look this term? I mean, I know you just love to try to be noticed, but isn't this a little bit extra, even for you?"

"Nice to see you too, Nel," Harley said, smiling unabashed. "Haven't you brought your every-help-bot with you? What's her name?"

"Who, Flo? Mum insisted we let her choose a name after all that business with the robots and the Iron Forest. It's daft, if you ask me. Anyway, why would I bring her with me? We're too old to be playing with robots."

"You're too old for fun?" Harley resisted the temptation to roll her eyes.

A shiny transporter chugged up the drive towards school. It was the type of vehicle for two that was fashionable in Inventia City, while in Forgetown people mostly got about by foot or on a trundle bike like Grandpa Eden's. Cosmo bundled out, looking a little embarrassed, wearing a T-shirt bearing the words "I love plants", and Harley smiled to herself. She had given him the shirt as a birthday present a couple of weeks ago. He looked over and waved before his mum kissed him goodbye and then sped off.

"See, Cosmo doesn't have a robot pet with him," Fenelda said, giving Harley the side-eye. "It's so refreshing to have another mature member in the year group. Someone much more on my level."

Harley let Fenelda's comment pass again, but she knew Cosmo would love a robot pet; his mum just didn't allow it.

Cosmo hurried over and Harley ran to give him a hello hug.

"I'm so excited I might burst!" Harley cried.

"Me too!" said Cosmo.

But before they could say any more, they were interrupted by a rumbling sound. Something extraordinary was coming up the path: a tri-wheeled trundle bike shaped like a dinosaur skeleton, the tail attached to the wheel at the back and with two legs at the front! Harley and Cosmo's jaws dropped open.

"That looks like a small version of the

Tyrannosaurus rex from the library book!" Harley said, agog.

The trundle bike was being driven by a woman sitting on top, a green cape flowing behind her and a bonnet shielding her face from the sun, pedalling away as the cogs and chains whirred beneath her.

Coming to a stop, she jumped down beside Harley and Cosmo, looked up at the clock on the tower of Cogworks and smiled.

"Wow, is that a real T-rex skeleton?" Harley asked.

The woman looked down at her with keen, shrewd eyes and a confident smile. "It's a model, adapted to a bike. Rather fun, don't you think?"

Harley nodded eagerly.

"Its full name is, of course, *Tyrannosaurus rex*, which means King of Tyrant Lizards."

"King of Tyrant Lizards," Harley repeated in awe, trying to push the picture of Professor Fretshaw out of her head.

Professor Spark strode down the Cogworks steps in her midnight-blue star dress. "Professor Anning! Welcome back. It's so good to see you again." Professor Spark was Harley's favourite teacher at

Cogworks because she was always kind and fair and set the most inventive projects.

"And you, Professor Spark," Professor Anning said, shaking hands.

"I see you've met Harley and Cosmo, two of my brightest young sparks."

A glow filled Harley inside to hear Professor Spark say that, but she still felt that she hadn't yet proven herself: she still hadn't won Pupil of the Term.

The other children quickly gathered round, also looking in awe at the amazing dino trundle bike.

"All the equipment you sent ahead has been packed on to the trackless train. It'll be myself and Professor Horatio accompanying you."

Professor Anning gave a nod. "Excellent. Then let's get the pupils aboard and head to the Jurassic Coast!"

CHAPTER 3
INVENTIA
JURASSIC COAST

After everyone had raced to the train, Harley and Cosmo bundled into one of the carriages with Letti and Asma. They sat with their robot pets on their laps, Sprocket half on Cosmo's lap because Harley didn't want him to feel left out. They zoomed through the Inventia landscape, first past the Iron Forest and the Junkyard of Forgotten Machine Dreams, then onwards through the farmlands, the Periscope

Lakes, and past Steelbury. At Buckle Bridge they stopped for lunch, which consisted of cog-shaped sandwiches, lemon fizz, fruit, and shortbread shaped like small hammers, which the Cogworks cook thought would be a fun way of getting them all in the fossil-excavating mood.

The trackless train and its excited inhabitants continued on through the long stretch of hills known as Glimmer Garden, which Cosmo told them was named after the silver-petalled daisies that made the hills glimmer in summer. Then on past Astroville, Chiselton, Dobbin Hollow and the Umber Caves, until finally, as the sun set and cast her bold summer palette of purples and pinks across the land, the town of Iron Regis and the cliffs of Inventia Jurassic Coast came into view.

"Wow, this is something else!" said Harley, jumping from the train. Her legs felt as though

...ded a good run after the long trip, and she ...ed she could go straight out to the sandy beach in front of them. The town was pretty, with colourful bunting suspended between stone houses and shops. Fishing boats bobbed happily in the harbour, and somewhere in the distance a lighthouse rhythmically flashed its beacon into the incoming evening.

"We'll have time for looking around tomorrow," said Professor Spark. "Right now we need to settle in for our late-evening meal and get a good night's sleep. Professor Anning has a big day planned for you. The Rock Hotel is just up this road here."

The hotel was a welcoming place with low ceilings, wood-cladded walls and all manner of ship paraphernalia, such as bells and wheels, adorning the walls, beside drawings of various sea creatures. The children were all sleeping in bunks arranged in two large rooms. Well, they had *eventually* fallen asleep, anyway, after what had seemed like hours of excited, whispered conversations after lights out.

*

The next morning, Professor Anning gave the class instructions over a breakfast of cereal and croissants with summer fruit jam in the dining room.

"Today, I shall be taking you to a special beach a little way from here. I have always been lucky finding fossils there, and I hope some of you will be too. For those who don't know, fossils are the remains of ancient life that have been preserved by natural processes. Can anybody tell me what we might find?"

Fenelda's hand shot up, and Harley's wasn't far behind.

Professor Anning indicated to Fenelda.

Fenelda flashed Harley a sly grin. "We might find the fossilized bones of animals, and their teeth, or shells. Maybe claws."

"Good," said Professor Anning. "But what else?"

Fenelda frowned, and Cosmo's eyes lit up as he raised his hand and then said, "Plants too. We might find fossilized leaves."

"Excellent!" Professor Anning took a small rock from her pocket and held it up for everyone to see. "This is an ammonite." She passed it around the class, and the students looked in wonder at the strange spiral imprint. "Ammonites were strange creatures that died out sixty-six million years ago." She took another rock from her pocket and gave that to them too.

"What is it?" asked Asma.

"Look carefully as you pass it round. Maybe one of you will work it out."

"I can't see any bones or teeth," said Henry, giving it to Letti.

"Maybe there's a claw inside?" Letti said, handing it to Harley.

"Wait – is the whole thing some sort of shell?" Harley asked, cupping the bobbly ball of rock in her hand and peering closely.

"It's a coprolite," said Professor Anning. "Or, in simpler terms, fossilized dinosaur poop."

Harley's eyes widened and she resisted the urge to drop it on the table. Opposite her, Fenelda sniggered, and beyond Cosmo, Rufus belly-laughed and said, "Pass it on, Harley, I've got to see this!"

Cosmo refused to touch the fossil, so Harley reached over and handed it to Rufus ... then quickly wiped her hands on her dungarees.

Professor Anning smiled. "It's not dinosaur poop any more, just the trace of it. The most important thing for you to remember today is that there are two types of fossils: body fossils and trace fossils. Body fossils are animal and plant remains, like teeth, shells, bones and leaves. Trace fossils are evidence left behind by animals, so things like footprints and poop!"

Professor Spark entered the dining room. "I've collected the packed lunches, so are we all ready to leave for the day?"

The class nodded eagerly and headed for the door.

After collecting their gear and their robot pets, the children were all given hard hats as they set off along the beach towards the cliffs, Professor Anning leading the way. Harley was glad of her sturdy boots for the rocky parts, while Sprocket leaped across the beach with ease, barking happily. It was a long trek, and it took about an hour to get to the spot the professor had in mind.

When they stopped, Professor Anning showed them the variety of tools that a fossil hunter might need: small hammers, chisels, steel points, brushes, magnifying glasses, gloves and safety goggles (although Harley had most of these on her tool belt already). After giving them some instructions and a demonstration, Professor Anning told them they were free to explore the area and see what they could find.

Harley and Cosmo went off together.

"OK, there's no ice-cream van here, but this is still a fun start to the term. To think we might find a dinosaur bone! Imagine what it must have been like here, so long ago…"

"How big do you think the plants were back then? As big as some of the dinosaurs?" Cosmo asked.

"Maybe!"

Ahead, Sprocket began digging in the pebbles.

"Have you found something, boy? Digging for a big bone?" Harley asked hopefully.

Cosmo laughed. "I wouldn't put too much on it; Sprocket will dig anywhere, just for the love of digging!"

Harley sighed. "You're probably right."

"Remember, Professor Anning advised us to look for regular marks and patterns," he said, putting his goggles on over his glasses.

They searched and searched. The odd cry of glee came from across the beach as student after student found something: a few spotted small ammonites; Letti found a tiny fossilized bone; Rufus was convinced a boulder he'd found was a huge T-rex poop, even though Professor Anning told him it most certainly wasn't; and just before lunch, Fenelda ran

32

over to Harley to boast that she'd found a tooth.

"It's an ichthyosaur tooth. Professor Anning told me. She said it was *very impressive*. What have you got?" Fenelda asked, knowing full well that they hadn't found anything yet.

But at that moment, Cosmo was quietly examining a small rock, and he suddenly declared, "It's a leaf!"

Fenelda patted him on the back. "Hmm. Not quite as impressive as a tooth, though, is it?" She skipped off.

Harley hurried to have a look with Cosmo. "Don't listen to Fenelda. It's amazing. Look, you can see the tiny details, and just think how old it is!"

As Professor Spark gathered everyone back together for lunch, Harley's heart sank a little. She still hadn't found anything, not even a hint of a fossil!

Sandwiches and drinks were handed out, and

Sprocket hopped around, popping ice out of his compartment for everyone.

Professor Anning sat with Harley and Cosmo. "We have another hour or so, then we must head back. Have you had fun so far?"

They both nodded.

"Although I wish I'd found something," said Harley, finding it harder and harder to hide her disappointment.

"You sometimes need a lot of patience, and even then it's not always enough." Professor Anning smiled. "But Cosmo's found a great fossil. I believe it's part of a tree from the Jurassic period. Perhaps an ancient predecessor of the needle pines of the Iron Forest by the shape of these leaves."

"Amazing!" breathed Cosmo, staring at his rock. Then he looked up. "Professor, I've been wondering: why is the beach a good place to find fossils?"

"Great question, Cosmo," Professor Anning said, beaming at him. "It's because most fossil formation happens after an animal dies in a watery environment and is buried in mud. Otherwise, their bodies would decay too quickly and not leave any trace. Also, fossils can be washed ashore from other places."

"Well, I'm not beaten yet!" said Harley standing up, determined to find her fossil, even if it might be as small as a hair.

They searched on, Harley looking intently as she clambered up and down the rocks on the beach. She felt dizzy from all the intense staring, but she didn't give up.

However, after another hour, Professor Anning called out a warning that they only had ten minutes left. Harley slumped down, defeated.

Fenelda passed by, nearly skipping, and gloated,

"Aw, better luck next time!"

"She knows very well that there is no next time," Harley harrumphed to Cosmo.

"You can share mine?" said Cosmo, holding his rock out to her.

Harley shook her head. "Thanks, that's very kind. But you found it, so you should take all the credit."

Sprocket whimpered and tilted his head.

"OK, OK, Sprocket, you've been patient enough all day. Let's have quick game of beach powerball before we have to head back."

Harley, Cosmo and Sprocket spread out a little further down the beach. Sprocket shot the ball out of his mouth, and Harley leaped to catch it, throwing it straight back so that Sprocket had to spring two metres into the air to catch it. Then he shot it to Cosmo, who fumbled and dropped it before returning it.

"Give me your most challenging ball, Sprocket. Full power!" Harley called.

Sprocket fired the ball like a missile, and Harley sprang out of the way. It belted into the rocks behind her. "Wow! Remind me to adjust your power down just a little," she said, laughing as she went to retrieve the ball.

"Time to head back, everyone!" shouted Professor Spark.

But Harley was frozen to the spot, staring in absolute amazement at the rocks where the ball had hit. The rock had split, revealing something extraordinary.

CHAPTER 4

THE FOSSIL

Harley put her goggles on and beckoned urgently to Cosmo and Sprocket.

"I think I've found something!"

Pulling on her gloves, she yanked at the piece of cracked rock to get a closer look. More of it came into view. Her heart rate rose. "Sprocket, shine your torch eyes into the gap." The light glared between the rocks, and she gasped. Surely it couldn't be?

"What is it?" Cosmo asked.

"I think it's a dinosaur footprint. A big one!"

"Harley, Cosmo!" called Professor Spark. "Time to go!"

"Just a minute, I may have found something!" Harley shouted, stalling for time. She grabbed the hammer and chisel from her belt. "Look. The rock has cracked almost all the way. If I can chip away a little here, it should…"

With a crack, half of the rock fell to the ground, revealing one huge, intact dinosaur footprint.

"Whoa!" Harley gasped.

By now half the class had caught on that something exciting was going on and hurried over, followed by the professors.

"It's huge!" exclaimed Cosmo.

Harley couldn't believe her luck. "Do you think it could be a T-rex footprint?"

Professor Anning put her hand on Harley's shoulder. "Well, well! What have you found?"

"A … footprint. It's a trace fossil," Harley said, remembering what the professor had told them earlier.

"Quite right. But this is truly amazing, Harley. Count the toes."

"Er, there seem to be six." Harley tried to remember which dinosaur it must be from the book she had read, but she hadn't been paying particular attention to how many toes each one had.

"A *Tyrannosaurus rex* only has three toes," said Professor Anning, whipping out her magnifying glass to examine the imprint more closely. "Some dinosaurs had four, and I can think of only one with five, but none with six! And the shape of the claw is unusual."

"Oh." Harley felt a pang of disappointment. Perhaps she hadn't found a dinosaur footprint after all.

Professor Anning looked up. "My dear, do you know what this means?"

Harley shook her head.

"It means you may have discovered a new species!"

Excited sparks tingled Harley's fingers and toes. "A new species?" she gasped.

"Perhaps!" said Professor Anning, her smile as wide as Harley's.

After unloading her tool trolley and distributing the equipment into various bags, Professor Anning and Professor Spark carefully lifted the fossilized footprint on top. The combined power of the super-strong robot pets meant that they could pull the large fossil footprint back across the beach, with Harley leading the way triumphantly.

Professor Anning chatted eagerly about the possibilities, but she was fairly sure the fossil just didn't match anything in historical records.

Fenelda Spiggot stomped along a little way away from the group and kept giving Harley narrow-eyed glares with tight lips.

"Perhaps I'll be handing this over to you at the end of term," Letti told Harley, patting the gold light-bulb badge pinned to her T-shirt.

Harley smiled. "There's still a long way to go this term. Anything could happen." But, in truth, she felt a glow inside, because she'd also had that thought. Surely such an important discovery made Pupil of the Term a fair certainty.

Two days later, Harley's claw-print fossil had been positioned in pride of place in the Cogworks entrance hall beside a huge, fossilized ammonite that Professor Anning had found on a previous dig. After making their way up the moving stairs to their classroom, Harley and Cosmo sat at the back of the class.

"It's going to be hard to come back down to earth after such an exciting start to the term," said Harley, who felt like a celebrity from the way her classmates were still chattering about her find.

"I know. I hope Professor Anning can find some information about what your dinosaur might have been like."

"Me too." She was itching to find out what this huge, six-footed wonder looked like, what it ate, how it lived…

Professor Spark had just finished taking the register when Professor Fretshaw, the head teacher, strode into the room. She stood at the front and observed them with haughty, wrinkly eyes.

"Excuse me for the interruption, Professor Spark. I wanted to congratulate you all on your recent finds on your field trip. I hear it was a great success."

"Indeed," said Professor Spark proudly.

"I've come to remind you about Pupil of the Term. While some of you may have stumbled upon some remarkable fossils, the honour of Pupil of the Term is given to pupils exhibiting remarkable achievements and commitment across the term. It is not a prize based on … luck. There is still a long way to go, and I shall be keeping a close eye on every one of you."

Her gaze met Harley's for a moment. Professor Fretshaw had always been tough on Harley, and always seemed to be waiting for Harley to mess up, but Harley managed to hold her head high and ignore it. And Professor Fretshaw was right: Harley's fossil find was amazing, but it had been a chance find, and she'd need to do more to prove herself. She'd let Pupil of the Term slip through her fingers too many times, and she wasn't going to do it again.

Professor Fretshaw left the room and Professor

Spark stood up.

"Right, class," she said. "It seems like a good time to announce your big project for the term."

Harley sat up straight. This project would be her chance to *really* prove herself.

"As it's the last term of the school year, I wanted to come up with something a little different, something that would bring out the best in you and allow you to pull together all the things you've learned."

The class exchanged glances, wondering what it could possibly be.

"Well, I concluded that the best approach was going for the most straightforward thing I could think of. The competition this term is to simply create your 'greatest invention'!"

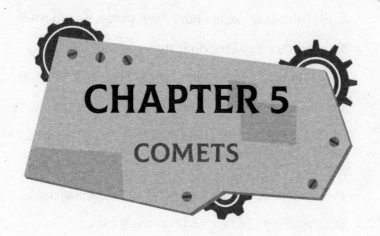

CHAPTER 5

COMETS

The class was abuzz with possibilities.

Professor Spark settled them down. "Now, everyone, we're going to spend the rest of the lesson thinking of inventions. While your idea could be absolutely anything, it should solve a problem, big or small. The quieter problems can be just as valid and make a big impact, so don't discount anything."

They began brainstorming ideas, but Harley's

mind kept drifting to the fossil footprint. "I wonder if the dinosaur might have had wings. Or maybe climbed trees and used all those toes to hold on to the branches."

Cosmo looked up. "You should be concentrating."

"I know, but do you think it was as big as a *Tyrannosaurus rex*?"

"Maybe. It *is* a big footprint. But do some work; you're going to get us told off in a minute!" Cosmo looked back at his sketchpad, where he was drawing what appeared to be the Cogworks school clock.

"But I have so many ideas I don't know which to choose. What are you doing?"

"It's inspired by you, actually, and the slug incident last year. I was thinking of creating some garden gnome robots to detect where the slugs are and ethically transport them away from the school lettuces."

"That's a good idea. Grandpa Eden would like that too! But they don't…"

"Don't what?"

"They don't exactly look like gnomes."

"That's because I'm designing them to look like knights. They're going to be Knights of the Slug Realm!"

They exchanged a look and sniggered.

"What about you?" Cosmo asked.

"I can't concentrate! I keep thinking about the claw print. I wish I could go back in time and find out what the dinosaur looked like. Maybe then I could design some sort of dinosaur riding saddle!"

"Yes, well, then you'd need a time-travel machine, and that's impossible."

"There must be *some* way of figuring out what it was like…"

Professor Spark stood before them. "Harley, I

would have expected a little more from you by now."

"Sorry, Professor," she mumbled.

Professor Spark's expression softened. "Your fossil *is* a very exciting discovery. But you still need to focus. Professor Anning is doing all she can to find out more for you. Keep your chat about your task, please."

Harley muttered an apology and looked back at her paper. She started sketching an imaginary dinosaur with a saddle.

"Harley, you poor thing." Fenelda was standing over Harley's desk. "So obsessed with that fossil, you can't think straight! And wouldn't it just be *awful* if it turns out not to be a fossil at all?"

Harley's eyes narrowed. "What do you mean?"

Fenelda shrugged and smiled sweetly. "Oh, you know, sometimes a rock is just a rock with grooves in it. If there's no other evidence for a new kind of dinosaur, well … maybe you and your robot were just barking up the wrong tree, so to speak?"

"It *is* a real fossil!"

"Well," Fenelda said, "let's keep hoping that Professor Anning can find something more. It would be awful if you just brought back a bit of boulder to school for no reason!"

As Fenelda sauntered away giggling, Harley turned back to her drawing, her ears burning. *Of course it's a real fossil!* she thought to herself. *And I'll find some way to prove it and wipe that smirk off Fenelda's face.*

Harley drew herself riding on the dinosaur's back with Sprocket, under the night sky. She began drawing the stars – then stopped, and tapped her pencil. A thought blossomed.

"What is it?" Cosmo whispered.

"The stars have been around for millions of years.

Maybe *they'll* know about my dinosaur!" It was a great idea. "It looks like I'll be going to the star-chatter observatory this evening!"

The star-chatter observatory stood on a hill just outside Forgetown. It had been one of Harley's favourite places to go ever since she was a child. Looking above, there were so many stars, so many planets, in such a gigantic space that surely nothing was impossible?

Harley and Sprocket climbed the spiral steps and found Dr Orbit inside.

He waved from one of the telescopes. "Hello, Harley! You've chosen a great day to visit. Halley's Comet is in the west sky."

She hurried over to take a look and saw a bright shape in the distant night. As they tracked the coordinates, Ursa Major, flamboyant in her all-white ball gown, bristling with feathers and sparkling with glitter, came into view.

"Harley, dahr-ling! How are you?"

"I'm great, thank you. Dr Orbit was just showing me Halley's Comet."

"Oh, him." Ursa rolled her eyes. "Halley is such a diva. He thinks he's some sort of universal rock star, zooming in and taking over our skies every seventy-six years, blasting out his electric guitar."

Vega sped down to join her. "I rather like his music. It makes a change from the endless opera performances."

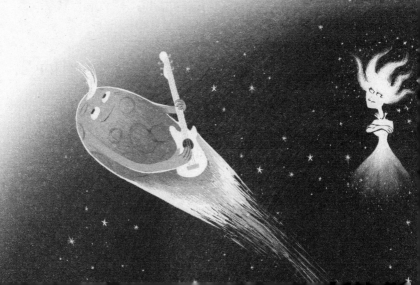

Ursa put her hand to her chest as though she'd been shot by something. "Vega! Wash your mouth out!"

Harley laughed.

"What's all the noise about?" Proxima Centauri zoomed down to them.

"Halley is playing guitar."

"I didn't know you'd taken up guitar, Harley?"

"*Halley,* not Harley, my dear, are you losing your hearing in your old age?" Ursa shook her head.

"Speaking of age, I have a question for you all," said Harley.

"Anything, Harley. Just name it," said Vega, smiling.

"You may have noticed we went on a school trip to Inventia Jurassic Coast."

Ursa nodded, sending sparkles of light shimmering around her head. "Of course we did.

Proxima was so jealous of the ice cream, weren't you, sugarplum?"

"I would do anything for a mint choc chip!"

"Well, I found a rather interesting fossil, and we can't identify it." Harley thought carefully about how to word the next part so that she didn't offend them. "And as you've been around for so many wondrous and prodigious years, I thought perhaps you might remember the dinosaurs?"

"Ah, yet another example of how comets are a nuisance," said Ursa. "Too busy playing their electric guitars to notice there's a whole planet in their path!"

"We do remember the dinosaurs," said Vega. "A little on the unglittery side for my liking, but remarkable nonetheless."

Harley's heart skipped a beat. She was suddenly a whisper away from finding out what her discovery was! "You don't happen to remember a *six-toed* dinosaur, do you?"

Ursa looked at Proxima, Proxima looked to the sky in thought, and Vega tapped his chin. They all frowned, then shrugged.

"Sorry, Harley. It was sixty-six million years ago," said Ursa.

"And we were really developing our talents then," said Proxima. "Some of our rehearsals lasted *decades*. We were very busy."

Harley's shoulders slumped. "It was a long shot, never mind."

"Now don't you look sad, sweetie pops!" said Ursa.

"Quick, let's cheer her up with a song," said Vega.

Proxima nodded. "There's a song for every occasion!"

"I have just the thing," Ursa whispered hurriedly to the other two stars. "A one, a two, a one two three—"

"Life, would be just fine, so fine.

Whoa, whoa,

If only we could turn back time."

Then a great guitar strum blasted across the sky, stopping them in their tracks.

Harley smiled. "Thank you for trying, but honestly, I'm not too sad. It's just a little frustrating, and I wish—" The thought came so clearly to her. "I wish I *could* turn back time." That was it! She needed to turn back time! To go and see for herself. Cosmo had even said it in class: *you'd need a time-travel machine, and that's impossible.*

But she was looking up at the stars, and nothing was impossible.

She was going to invent a time machine.

CHAPTER 6

VIOLET

The idea had planted itself firmly in Harley's mind, and once that happened, there was no going back. She was going to build a time machine. That way, she could go back and find her dinosaur for herself. Not only would she have invented an incredible machine that might change the world, but she could prove her fossil was real. *Take that, Fenelda!* And, of course, getting Pupil of the Term would be a certainty.

There was just one problem: she didn't know where to start.

There were three places that Harley liked to go for advice. One was her grandpas, always wise and kind, the second was the stars, with their unique vantage point in the sky, and the third was the Rusty River. On this occasion she thought the river would be the best starting point, so the next day, after sending a message to Sprocket to meet her at the school gates with a fishing rod, she hurried there. She wanted Cosmo to join her, but he'd just started helping out at the library after school so he couldn't make it.

Harley sat on the bridge, her legs dangling over the edge and cast her line. The water here always had an orange tinge to it because it flowed from the Copper Mountains to the east of Forgetown. It was a unique place where you could fish for inspiration. The various species of mechanical fish you might catch always had something wise to say. Harley had learned that they liked to be cryptic, and she would often misinterpret their advice, but at times it had proven to be incredibly useful. Most people thought it was nonsense – especially Fenelda Spiggot – but Harley liked the fact that most people didn't believe it, because this way she could have the river all to herself.

"Move over."

Harley jolted at the unexpected voice and looked up to see … Fenelda! "What are you doing here?" Harley asked, eyeing her suspiciously.

"None of your business." Fenelda sat down beside her.

Awkward silence hung between them as Harley sat, rod in hand, waiting for a fish, with Fenelda beside her.

"If you're trying to put me off or intimidate me, it's not going to work, Nel."

"Don't flatter yourself. I'm waiting."

"Waiting for a fish? I thought you didn't believe in their advice anyway, and you don't even have a rod. They don't just leap out into your arms, you know."

Fenelda gave Harley a pitying look. "I'm not waiting for a daft fish."

Harley shrugged. "Your loss."

Silence fell again. Sprocket gave the odd awkward whine, and Harley prayed that her fish would hurry up.

Suddenly something zoomed past Harley's ear. She wobbled and tried not to fall into the river. "What in all Inventia was that? Was it a *pigeon*?"

Ahead, the bird zoomed onwards towards the Junkyard of Forgotten Machine Dreams.

"Useless. Just as I thought," said Fenelda,

scribbling something in her notepad.

"What are you up to, Nel?" Harley hated to admit it to herself, but she was now intrigued by whatever Fenelda was doing.

"Pigeon Post. I've been suspecting that there's a flaw in the mechanics of their homing device. I set that bird off at lunchtime with post for Inventia City, and it was meant to meet me back here, but it got confused and is now going who knows where."

Harley had heard Miss Li – of Forgetown's robot postal services – complain that she was always sending out search parties for missing pigeons.

"Small problems that have a big impact. My invention is for an effective homing device. An add-on mechanism that is going to help everyone in Forgetown with their post and will make so many other things more efficient. It's sure to bag me Pupil of the Term again. Sorry, Harley, I know you've been hoping to get it someday." Fenelda flashed her a false smile.

Harley hated to admit it, but it was a pretty good idea.

Just then, Harley's line tugged hard. "I've got one!" She reeled it in a little, but the pull was too powerful, and her rod strained under the pressure. Tugging again, the fish broke through the surface of the water: it was huge, flat and had broad fins. Harley had never come across a fish like it.

She could feel herself slipping towards the edge of the bridge as they entered into a tug of war. If it was resisting this hard, Harley decided it *must* be the fish she needed. "Don't just stand there, Nel, help me!"

"But it's so fun watching you struggle."

"Nel!"

Fenelda tutted and grasped the rod alongside

Harley. It was the extra strength Harley needed, and with another pull, the fish sprang from the water and leaped towards them. Harley dropped the rod and stretched out her arms to grasp it.

The fish and Harley stared at each other. She could now see it was a manta ray.

"Sorry about that," it said in a squeaky voice. "I just wanted to make sure you were deserving of my advice."

Harley raised her chin. "I'm ready."

The robot manta ray cleared its throat. "Those who see further do so by standing on the shoulders of giants."

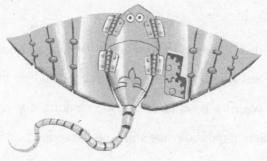

Majestically it leaped out of her hands and flipped backwards, landing with a splash in the waters below.

Fenelda sighed heavily. "I'll let you and your purple hair carry on with your little games, Harley. I'm off to do important work to win back Pupil of the Term for a third time, which will be…" She slowly counted to three on her fingers. "Three times more than you've won it."

Harley stood up and planted her hands on her hips. "Well, you can keep your pigeons, because *I'm* inventing something far more incredible."

"Let me guess: a whistle to finally control your little pet?"

Sprocket's eyes flashed yellow, and he growled.

"No! *Time travel.*" She knew that telling Fenelda her plan wasn't a good idea, but she couldn't stop herself trying to wipe the smug smile off Fenelda's face.

There was a long pause.

Then Fenelda burst out laughing.

Sprocket put his front paws over his eyes and whimpered.

"Time travel! I've heard it all now. Honestly, Harley. You are quite ridiculous." Still laughing and shaking her head, Fenelda started skipping away up the path. But Harley didn't care because the fish had given her all she needed. Fenelda could keep her postal pigeon homing device. Harley was going *big*.

For once, Harley knew exactly what the fish's advice had meant. In order to make a time-travel machine, she didn't have to do all the work herself. She would research all the inventors who'd tried to invent time-travel machines before her, and simply pick up where they had left off, filling in the missing pieces!

Her next port of call was Cosmo, who at that

moment was exactly where she needed him to be: at Forgetown Library.

"And Nel!" Harley called after her. "The shade of my hair is *violet*, actually!"

CHAPTER 7
THE TIME MACHINE

"Cosmo!"

"Harley? I thought you were going to the Rusty River?"

"I did, and it worked, and now I need you to help me find the most recent books on time travel. You know this library like the back of your hand. Can you help?"

"But I told you before, time travel is impossible."

"Says who? Besides, I thrive on impossible."

"Or at least very dangerous."

"Do you think any inventor who achieved anything was put off by a little risk?" Harley waved her hand as though it was of no consequence. "Are you going to help me find the books, or not?"

"You're going to do it anyway, so I may as well help you."

"That's the spirit!"

Harley left the library with an armful of books and another pile strapped to Sprocket's back. Most of them seemed off-topic to Harley, but Cosmo insisted she take everything that had even a vague connection to the science of time travel.

He'd also made her promise to read every single one, so it was three weeks before she started actually building her machine. She worked furiously in her room at Hitch House in every spare moment that she got. She barely saw Cosmo, unless he popped by to help her, but he was mostly busy working on his Knights of the Slug Realm.

It was halfway through the term when Harley started to make real progress. She'd designed her time-travel machine to look like a large backpack with straps that hooked over your shoulders. Inside were numerous cogs, wires and components that she'd had to order from companies in Inventia. There was an adjustable date display and various instruments and gauges.

Every school day Harley would check in on her fossil footprint, which was still on display in the Cogworks entrance hall. Harley's find had attracted a lot of interest and controversy, and scientists were coming from all over Inventia to see the unusual six-toed fossil for themselves. But still no one had an answer for what it could possibly be, and there was a growing number of voices saying that it might not be a fossil at all. But seeing it every day reminded Harley how important it was to keep going on her machine, no matter how hard it was, and that soon she would be able to go back in time and see the amazing creature for herself. She'd take some photographs as evidence and present them to the school – and prove Fenelda wrong.

Every weekend was dedicated to working on her invention. Sprocket was proving useful as he would rush off to the Iron Forest for Harley every time she needed a different cog size. She was eagerly counting down to test day.

Grandpa Elliot asked her the same question every teatime: "What is it you're working on up there?"

"You know she won't tell us. She always just says

'it's a surprise!'" said Grandpa Eden.

Harley smiled. "It *is* a surprise. But I'm getting close."

"At least Cosmo's not being so secretive," said Grandpa Eden. "I think he's on to something with his Knights of the Slug Realm, so I've asked him to build me one for the greenhouse.

It wouldn't surprise me if he won Pupil of the Term again."

Grandpa Elliot passed freshly baked rolls around the table. "I bumped into Mrs Spiggot at Kitchen Imagine and she delighted in telling me how Fenelda's developing a homing device that will revolutionize post in Inventia. I'm afraid you'll have to go some way to top the other pupils, Harley."

"Don't worry. I'm going to smash it."

Her grandpas exchanged a glance.

"That's what we're worried about," muttered Grandpa Eden.

"Have faith, grandpas. I'm testing it this weekend, and there's nothing to worry about."

It was Sunday morning: test day. As her initial test, Harley had decided to time-travel only a short distance, back to the day before. Her plan was to start by travelling back in short bursts of time, and then, as her tests progressed, she would make her way back to Jurassic times, sixty-six million years ago.

Cosmo sat on Harley's bed, wringing his hands.

"Stop it, you're making me feel nervous," said Harley.

"But you might be the first person to explode attempting time travel!"

"All right, Mr Worry Pants."

"Well, you've given me good reason to worry this time! What if you see yourself and accidentally create some sort of parallel world? We don't know what happens when someone's timeline loops around like that! What if you break time itself?"

"Look, I'm only going back to yesterday. Remember when I called for you in Hinge Street? That's where we'll both be. I'll arrive back here in my bedroom, and I won't risk seeing my past self because I know I wasn't here; I was with you."

Harley set the dial on the numerical calendar to the day before, then eased the time-travel machine over her shoulders. It was extremely heavy, and she buckled at the knees for a moment, then straightened up.

"Hold on to your hat, Cosmo." Her finger hovered over the activate switch on her shoulder.

Then she pressed it.

CHAPTER 8

NOTHING

A whirr sounded and a pulse of power propelled Harley forward. She managed to throw her hands out to prevent smashing her nose into the floor.

Hastily, she looked around, her heart pounding her ribs. Had it worked?

"Harley, you're a liability," said Cosmo.

She pushed herself up and looked over her shoulder. "You're still here?"

"Er, yeah, just about." He straightened his skew-whiff glasses.

"Sprocket, could you show the date, please? Sprocket?"

The robot dog crawled out from under the bed with a whimper and flashed the date in his digital eyes.

"Ah, it's still today." Harley's mood sank. The test had failed. "Sorry if I scared you both. Something must've gone a bit wrong."

"Do you think?" Cosmo said, shaking his head in disbelief.

"All right, no need to get sassy with me." Harley pushed herself up and straightened out her clothes. "Every invention has hiccups."

"That was more than a hiccup."

"What's all the crashing?" called Grandpa Elliot from downstairs.

"Nothing! Everything's fine. We were just playing powerball with Sprocket," Harley called.

Cosmo shook his head again, disapproving of her lie. "I have a really bad feeling about all of this…"

"The machine obviously needs a few adjustments. Let's meet the same time tomorrow at your house."

"My house! Why can't we just try again here?"

"Because we'll both have been here and can't risk seeing ourselves, silly. You know, the whole breaking time thing?"

"Oh, right. But you'd better sort out whatever just went wrong, because my mum won't be happy with loud crashing noises."

Harley spent the rest of the evening going over her calculations and making adjustments. She was disappointed the first test run hadn't gone to plan as the term was flying by, but she told herself that every great inventor had to overcome challenges. She wolfed down her tea and worked late into the night.

The next day, she packed her time-travel machine into her large rucksack and hurried downstairs with Sprocket.

Her grandpas were chatting in the kitchen.

"I'm going to Cosmo's to work on our projects together. See you later!"

"Don't you want breakfast?" Grandpa Elliot asked, striding into the hall, an arm outstretched with a plate of fruit pastries.

"Ooh, thanks!" Harley grabbed one and opened the front door.

A fern smacked her in the face. "What has Grandpa Eden been planting?" She peered out into a barrage of green foliage.

Grandpa Elliot looked as perplexed as her. "Eden, I think you've planted these ferns a bit too close to

the door."

"What ferns?" asked Grandpa Eden, walking into the hallway. His mouth dropped open in shock. "Harley, have you been at my super-grow formula again?"

"After the slug? Most definitely not."

Grandpa Eden scratched his head. "Perhaps Daisy spilled some near the door." Daisy was their mechani-weather-bot who helped in the greenhouse.

Harley pushed her way outside through the leaves. It was like a jungle had surrounded the front door, but she couldn't let Daisy's mishaps interrupt her plans for the day. She left her two puzzled grandpas and hurried along the path in the direction of Forgetown, looking back to see that a tangle of thick vines had travelled up the walls of Hitch House overnight too. *Strange,* she thought.

But no matter: the morning was bright and

clear and full of hope. Today was going to be the day – or if her machine worked, today was going to be yesterday! Keen to get to Cosmo's quicker to try her machine again, she decided to hold on to Sprocket's lead and activate his turbo-boost legs. As they zoomed around the bend, Sprocket yelped and veered to the side and Harley threw herself out of the way of a woman dressed in a voluminous purple dress and a sparkling crown.

Harley tumbled into the grass verge. Brushing herself down, she looked back at the woman.

"Mind thy way, mistress!" the woman said abruptly.

"Oh, sorry," said Harley, wondering why she was speaking so strangely. Perhaps she was from a different part of Inventia. "Er, are you lost?"

But the woman continued walking, looking as though she was searching for something.

Harley shrugged. Perhaps there was a fancy-dress party going on in town; Mr Bobbins at Cosmic Sewing liked to celebrate occasions like Halloween or Christmas with a fancy-dress party. But at this time of year … perhaps it was his birthday? The lady was probably heading there, Harley decided.

"Town is in this direction!" she called, but the woman just carried on.

Harley shrugged. "Perhaps we'll leave the turbo boost off for now, Sprocket."

They continued along the country lane towards Hinge Street, but after a short distance they passed a large bush and heard rustling. They paused and warily peered into the leaves.

Then a man in full, old-fashioned armour sprang from the bushes!

"Aargh!" Harley yelled.

Sprocket went into defence mode and began a

flurry of robotic barks.

The soldier eyed them suspiciously over his shield, holding his sword up with his other hand.

"Ah, I see," Harley said, suddenly realizing that this person must be on their way to Mr Bobbins' fancy-dress party too. He seemed to have made a great effort – his iron helmet and body armour looked authentic – so she supposed it made sense that he was so committed to his character.

"*ubi est castellum?*" he said gruffly.

Harley nodded, not understanding a word. "Hmm, yes, very good. Have fun at the party!"

She turned and headed up Hinge Street; she couldn't help but wonder how that party would be any fun if everyone kept acting so strangely.

CHAPTER 9
TEST RUN TWO

"Morning, Cosmo! Ready for Test Run Two?"

"I'm not sure I'll ever be ready for your test runs, but come inside. Mum's gone out."

"Has she gone to Mr Bobbins' fancy-dress party?"

Cosmo frowned. "Er, no."

They walked through Cosmo's hall, which was full of boxes. For a moment, Harley's stomach tied itself in a knot. "You're not moving again, are you?!" she cried.

"Oh, no! Don't worry, Mum likes it here in Forgetown. These boxes are kind of your fault, actually."

"My fault?"

"Mum's persuaded the council that we should create a mini natural history museum here in Forgetown on account of your find. She thinks it might bring in lots of tourists, so she wants to convert the empty shop next to Picante's Pizza Parlour. These are boxes of things that people have donated so far."

One of the boxes was open. Harley noticed a palm-sized, off-white egg nestled in straw. "This must be a mistake – there's an egg in here."

"No, it's meant to be there. It's Mum's first piece. Apparently, it's the last egg of some bird called a dodo. Her friend Marjorie from Inventia has lent it to her."

"Do you think it'll hatch?" Harley asked, leaning in expectantly.

"Not likely. It's over three hundred years old."

"When I get my time machine to work, we won't need a museum. We can turn the shop into a time-travel agency and send people to see for themselves!"

"Sure, Harley," Cosmo said with a smile.

Cosmo's room was filled with greenery, and there were library books stacked on every bit of surface that didn't have a plant.

Harley took out her time-travel machine, carefully adjusted the date to the previous day and heaved it on to her shoulders. "Right. If all goes well, you'll be at mine chatting with me and about to embark on Test Run One, and I'll end up back here in your room on my own."

"Wait, what if you bump into Mum? Which of course you won't because the chances of you getting this machine to work are like a million to one, but, say you do, she'll wonder what the diddles you're doing here."

"A million to one, you say? But I thought you said time travel was impossible?" she teased. "I guess I'll figure that out when I get there. Ready?"

"As I'll ever be."

She braced herself and pressed the button. It felt like being hit in the back by a huge wave. Harley face-planted into Cosmo's bed as a *whoosh* passed her ears. She lay there for a moment, her ears ringing.

"That was more powerful than the last time!" she exclaimed. Excited bubbles fizzled inside her. Had it worked?

"Still here," groaned Cosmo, who was splayed on the floorboards.

Harley tried not to let the disappointment get her down. She pushed herself up and took off the time-travel machine backpack. "There's obviously something missing." Maybe she should try the Rusty River again? Or go back to the library, or—?

"Come on," she said decisively. "We're going to the Iron Forest."

The Iron Forest was unlike anywhere else in Inventia because it grew all sorts of mechanical equipment, such as springs, cogs and nails, but it seemed to have the uncanny knack of knowing what was needed and occasionally grew more unusual things, like the time it grew a full wheelbarrow just when Grandpa Eden's had broken. Perhaps it would grow Harley what she needed for the machine.

Cosmo sighed and nodded. "All right, sure. I could do with a couple of springs for the final touches to my gnome knights."

They left Cosmo's house and hurried along the path to the Iron Forest, chatting about their

inventions. As they rounded the corner, something
hit Harley in the shoulder.

"Ow!" she said, rubbing her shoulder. She looked

down to see what had hit her: a robotic postal pigeon. It twitched once on the ground, then took flight again.

Then a voice called out, "Come back, stupid bird!"

Fenelda stomped after the pigeon, which was dancing in strange angles around the sky.

"Is your homing device not going to plan?" Harley asked, trying not to give in to the smug feeling rising in her chest.

"It was, until just now!" Fenelda harrumphed.

"It's only two weeks until we present our inventions," Harley said. "I do hope you can perfect it by then."

"I'll have you know, I *have* perfected it. I had the pigeon in rest mode when I turned my back for a moment; then when I looked back, some daft *giant bird* began pecking my pigeon like it was a great nut!"

"Giant bird?" Cosmo asked quizzically.

"That's what I said. Some waist-high monstrosity. Then it disappeared into the Iron Forest." Fenelda waved in the general direction.

"Attacking a pigeon? It was probably just a large ironhog," suggested Harley. "Or a velocipede."

"I think I can recognize a bird when I see one, thank you. I'll have to sort out the dent before I present it to Professor Spark now." Fenelda sighed, then narrowed her eyes at Harley. "Anyway, what's in that huge backpack?"

"It's full of none of your business."

"You're not still persisting with that ludicrous time-travel idea, are you?" Fenelda shook her head and put a pitying hand on Harley's arm. "There's still time to choose something realistic and achievable, you know. Something a little more within your … *ability*."

Harley felt her blood start to boil. She knew Fenelda relished winding her up, and most of the time she could ignore it, but on this occasion, she couldn't stop the words tumbling from her mouth: "Well, I think your idea is rubbish and boring. It's never going to get anywhere." Even as she said the words, she knew they were wrong. The truth was she didn't think Fenelda's idea was rubbish, it was her attitude that was.

Cosmo looked down and shuffled his feet awkwardly.

"If I want your opinion, I'll ask for it," said Fenelda haughtily.

"Likewise. You do you, I'll do me, and may the best girl win."

Cosmo coughed. "Or boy. Pupil of the Term isn't just about you two, you know."

They both looked at him, aghast, and his cheeks

blushed red.

Above the Iron Forest, a group of copper wagtails took flight in a sudden flurry. Harley frowned. It was probably the same ironhog that had attempted to eat Fenelda's robot pigeon. Or perhaps the forest was growing the mysterious part she needed for her machine!

"See you in class, Nel. I have work to do," Harley said and skipped towards the forest with Sprocket and Cosmo in tow.

CHAPTER 10

THIRD TIME LUCKY

Harley scoured the Iron Forest for any sign of something different, something that might be the missing part she needed. She rooted through cogweed, hunted under nailberry bushes and searched in the silvery leaves of the needle pines. Cosmo had collected the springs he needed, so he and Sprocket sifted through the undergrowth helping Harley.

"What exactly are we looking for?"

"Something super-looking." Then a thought struck her: "Perhaps it's something that future me will send back in time and place here to help past me! Because I might not be able to figure out the time machine now, but maybe I do in ten years' time or so, so I time-travel back and help the now me, which means I *do* figure it out now all along!"

"Harley, you're making my head spin."

"No, I'm on to something here! Maybe this is the moment I'm meant to figure it out, and it's, say, this simple-looking but slightly unusual purple cog here."

"I think you're putting two and two together and making five again."

"But look! It's the only purple cog amongst the yellow." She wiggled her eyebrows. "I'll go back home and add this to the machine, then we'll do Test Run Three tomorrow. Grandpa Eden's lucky number is three; I have a good feeling about this!"

"But tomorrow is a school day."

"Perfect! Because if I time-travel to the day before, there will be no one at school! I'll do the test early, before the other students arrive. Meet me there?"

Cosmo nodded reluctantly. "But Harley, perhaps Fenelda had a point…"

"I'm going to pretend I didn't hear you say that. We'll sneak in before Primbot mans the gates."

They said goodbye, and Harley hurried back to Hitch House to make her final adjustments. The giant ferns outside the front door had been cut back, but there were so many creepers that Grandpa Eden hadn't managed to remove even half of them in the time that Harley had been away.

When she arrived, Grandpas Elliot and Eden were talking in the kitchen.

"I've contacted the Horticultural Society, but nobody else seems to be having the same problem. It's most peculiar. All I can think is that some invasive new species has blown in on the wind."

"Very strange. You know, I've had a note from the office asking me to investigate some strange sightings. Something about two actors from out of town: a Roman soldier in full dress and a queen."

"Oh, those two were just going to Mr Bobbins' fancy-dress birthday party."

"Mr Bobbins? Isn't his birthday in winter?" asked Grandpa Eden.

Harley shrugged. "Anyway, I need to finish my project. I have a final test run to do. Presentations start in class tomorrow!" She hurried upstairs.

Harley didn't get much sleep that night. She was up late putting the final touches to her time-travel machine – including the new cog – and the excitement of the upcoming test run kept her from falling asleep.

She met Cosmo at the school gates before eight.

"Do you think, just once, we could have an explosion-free day?"

"Go big or go home! Who was it who said that?" She thought it must have been some sort of famous scientist or inventor. "Einstein, perhaps?"

"Or perhaps you just made it up. Harley, are you sure about this?"

"It's going to work this time. I can feel it in my bones." Harley paused on the school steps. "Although, perhaps we should do Test Run Three on the school lawn, just in case."

After carefully setting the dial to the day before, Harley pulled the time-travel machine on to her back and pressed the button for a third time.

The sonic wave that emanated from the machine propelled Harley several metres above the ground, the pressure waves pulsing through the air at great speed, making a booming sound like thunder. Prickles of electrical energy pulsed through Harley's body. Everything seemed to slow down and become a blur as she flew through the air and landed with a crash on the Cogworks lawn.

She lay there for a moment, unable to move, feeling the weight of the time-travel machine on her back, then the ringing in her ears finally cleared. She looked around for Cosmo and Sprocket.

They were gone! The fizzle of success made her jump up, despite the aches of the fall: *it had worked!*

There was no stopping her now. She paced from side to side, too excited to stay still. Should she go straight back sixty-six million years, or test it out on more recent history? She wished Cosmo or Sprocket

were there for advice, but what would it matter? She'd be away and then back to the future without them even realizing she'd gone!

A groan sounded in the bushes. "Harley!" Cosmo emerged, leaves and twigs sticking out of his curly hair and Sprocket in his arms.

Her shoulders slumped. "Oh no! It's still today, isn't it?"

"That blast almost knocked *me* into yesterday! Honestly, Harley, I stick by you through all your zany ideas, but I think it's my duty to stand up to you now and say—"

"ROAR!"

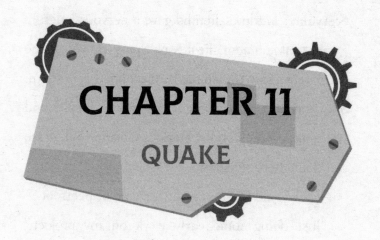

CHAPTER 11

QUAKE

Harley and Cosmo exchanged a look of utter confusion. The roar seemed to have come from somewhere behind the main Cogworks building.

"*What did you do?*" Cosmo asked in such a quiet, fearful voice that even Harley started to feel worried.

"It wasn't *me* that roared, if that's what you're thinking."

"Maybe we imagined it."

"Or maybe that's how Professor Fretshaw starts every day," Harley said, and gave a nervous laugh.

At that moment, Professor Spark drove up the drive in her blue transporter and stopped near them. She hurried out of the car, frowning deeply, and straightened the aerial. "Harley? Cosmo? What are you doing here so early?"

"Er—" said Cosmo, going a shade of beetroot.

"Just doing some early work on my project," Harley interrupted, and shot Cosmo a *don't say anything* look.

"Did you just feel the ground shake?"

"A little … I guess."

"Earthquakes in Forgetown? This is unheard of."

The main doors of the Cogworks building flew open, and Professor Fretshaw rushed down the steps. "Professor Spark! Did you experience the quake? I'm calling an emergency meeting. I've already sent a transmission to the other professors to get here as soon as possible."

Several loud thuds pulsed the ground.

"Sounds like aftershocks," declared Professor Fretshaw, doing a double take at Harley and Cosmo. "What are you two doing here so early?" She waved her hand as Harley opened her mouth to make up an excuse. "Never mind, I'm too busy. Make yourselves scarce."

The professors were in such a confusion over the quake that neither seemed to notice Harley's massive backpack, although Professor Spark turned back and flashed a fleeting glance of suspicion at them as she entered Cogworks.

"I think it's safe to say that Test Run Three didn't work," said Cosmo.

But Harley had a creeping feeling of dread trickling the length of her spine. It may not have worked, but *something* had happened. "Come on, we need to see what's going on around the back. Follow my lead, move with caution, and Sprocket, come with us. I have a feeling we'll need you."

Stealthily, Harley and Cosmo made their way around to the back of Cogworks.

"Perhaps it was just some freak thunder. You know, like some sort of sunny day electrical storm? The professors didn't seem to notice it."

"They were both inside something at the time so they might not have heard. And I don't think thunder can actually make the ground shake."

They rounded the building and froze at the sight before them.

It stood on two legs as thick as iron oaks and was the height of the Cogworks domed clock tower. A muscular body led up to a long, spiny neck, its arms sported striped, bat-like, webbed wings, its head had ice-blue eyes and a single crest. The spikes along its back were a vibrant purple, the scaly skin a light turquoise. Its tail whipped the air like a loose air hose, and its tongue lolled snakelike out of the side of its many-toothed jaw. Chilling silver claws reflected the morning sun.

Harley and Cosmo stood, utterly terrified and open-mouthed, as they attempted to make sense of what they were seeing. There was no mistaking its dinosaur-like appearance.

And by good fortune, it hadn't noticed them; its focus seemed to be on the shiny glass roof of Professor Horatio's Horticultural Studies greenhouse.

It hadn't noticed them *yet*.

"Harley, you're gaping like a Rusty River carp," Cosmo said in a hushed whisper. "Say something, or at least tell me I'm dreaming!"

But Harley had become transfixed by the

dinosaur's feet.

"Count them, Cosmo!" she said breathlessly. "It has six toes. It's *my dinosaur*!"

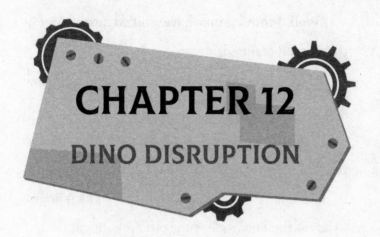

CHAPTER 12

DINO DISRUPTION

The moment of horror sent a chill through Harley's body, as though someone had cracked a dinosaur-sized, ice-filled egg over her head.

How could this be happening? *Her* dinosaur? Here?

Her brain whirled with thoughts, but one came to the fore: "You know I said Test Run Three didn't work?"

"Uh-huh," trembled Cosmo.

"Well, I think it may have worked, just … not in the way I'd planned."

"Harley, how does everything with you somehow end up 'off plan'?!"

"On the plus side, I think we have undoubtable proof of a new species of dinosaur."

Cosmo's pale face reddened with sudden anger. "And on the downside, your proof might eat us and the rest of Forgetown!"

Harley knew she had to think fast. When things went wrong, her grandpas always taught her to take a deep breath and think in practical steps.

Inhale, exhale.

So: first, she had to get the dinosaur away from Cogworks before the children started arriving – somewhere safe, where they could try to contain it. She couldn't risk going back to tell the professors because the dinosaur might run off, and they'd lose their chance to stop it causing trouble.

She looked down at Sprocket, who was sitting eagerly by her feet.

"Move silently," she said, pulling Cosmo back behind the wall, out of the dinosaur's view, and beckoning Sprocket to follow. She crouched down, and Cosmo did the same. "The dinosaur seems transfixed by shiny things, so what if—"

Before Harley could finish her thought, hot air blew over them, and there was a strange snorting noise. They looked up to see the ice-blue eyes of the dinosaur looking towards them, peering around the wall.

"Aaaargh!" they yelled.

Like arrows unleashed, they pelted towards the only route open to them. Hands flailing, Harley and Cosmo shouted and sprinted back past Cogworks and down the lane that led towards town.

After the first few moments of panicked fleeing, they slowly realized that there was no sound behind them, and they fell into focused silence as they ran.

But then, just as they wondered if they could be in the clear, there was a thud of hefty dinosaur footsteps behind them. Sprocket, who was ahead, unleashed a rope and some roller wheels from his back and Harley knew what to do.

"Quick, we'll share the wheels. Tie one over your boot, then grab my waist!"

He didn't hesitate. They looped the wheels over their feet, grasped the rope, and Sprocket set off on his turbo-zoom legs.

"Get to the safety of the buildings!" Harley called.

The town was still waking up and the shops weren't open yet, so the streets ahead looked to be empty.

"Any ideas for where we can hide while we come up with a plan?" shouted Harley, holding on as Sprocket sped forward. She was hoping that the inhabitants of Forgetown would stay inside so her dinosaur wouldn't eat them!

Cosmo perked up with a jolt, even as he strained to keep hold of the rope. "I know! The empty shop next to Piccanto's! It might not be locked because Mum said different teams of workers have been going in and out all week!"

Another great roar sounded behind. Every footstep the dinosaur made jolted through Harley as they slowed down at Piccanto's.

Praying Cosmo was right, Harley yanked at the neighbouring shop's door handle as the dinosaur followed them into the square.

The door flew open. "Quick! Inside!"

Several screams sounded through windows that

looked on to the square.

The dinosaur had come to a halt and was looking around with curiosity … and what looked to Harley to be *hunger*.

"We can't let it eat anyone! What if old Granny Crankett comes out for her morning stroll? She can barely see, even with her glasses on! It'll gobble her up in one bite." Harley drummed her fingers against the glass, thinking. "I know! Maybe we can lead it to the Horticultural Society and trap it inside?"

"Harley, it would never fit through the doors!"

Harley was thinking fast. She watched as the dinosaur became fixated on the shiny water fountain and bent to take a drink. "Or maybe… OK, I have a plan! But it's a risk, and I have no idea if it'll work."

"It's a plan more than I've got. What are you thinking?"

"From the little we've seen, the dinosaur seems

to be distracted by shiny things: the greenhouse roof at Cogworks, and now the fountain."

"Right?"

Harley turned to Sprocket. "I hate to ask this of you, but I can't think of anything else right now. We need to get the dinosaur to someplace with fewer people, somewhere shiny and enclosed."

"The Iron Forest!" exclaimed Cosmo, and Harley nodded.

"You're shiny, Sprocket. If you run in the direction of the Iron Forest using your turbo zoom, it might follow you. Once it's in the Iron Forest, it'll hopefully be transfixed by the trees, and we can work out what in all of Inventia to do next."

Sprocket let out a yap of agreement and his eyes flashed with light bulbs.

"He thinks it's a good plan!" Harley bent and stroked his head. "Be careful. Lead it up the east lane, which should be the furthest away from any people. Once you've taken the dinosaur far enough into the forest, turn all your lights off and head back and meet us at Cogworks. We need to find Professor Anning. If there's anyone who'll know what to do about a dinosaur on the loose, it's her."

Cosmo grabbed Harley's arm. "Hurry! Granny Crankett is over the other side of the square, and she hasn't seen a thing!"

Quick as a flash, Harley opened the door, and with a blast of light at his heels, Sprocket flew outside once more. The dinosaur turned its head to look at Granny Crankett.

"Make some noise!" Harley called.

Sprocket began barking on full volume, so that it reverberated from the walls of the square. The dinosaur swung its crested head to see, and its eyes lit up at the sight of the silver dog. With ferocious speed it lunged, but Sprocket's turbo zoom sent him flying across the square, the dinosaur in hot pursuit.

A ball of fear embedded itself in Harley's chest. "He will be all right, won't he?"

Cosmo nodded. "He'll be fine. You made him with your grandpas, and with all the improvements you've added over the years, there's no robo-dog like him."

The ball of fear grew bigger. "Oh! What if the dinosaur loses interest as it follows him … and it ends up at Hitch House?"

"It won't," Cosmo reassured her. "But we'd better get back to Cogworks and sort this out as quickly as possible."

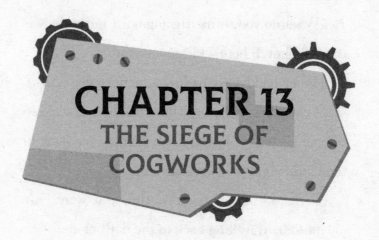

CHAPTER 13
THE SIEGE OF COGWORKS

"Good morning, Granny Crankett. Nice day for a stroll!" Harley said with an awkward laugh.

"Morning, Fenelda. Be careful today. I think I hear thunder."

The thuds of the dinosaur chasing Sprocket faded away.

"Fenelda?" Harley joked, as she ran with Cosmo back across the square. "I almost wish I hadn't saved her now!"

"What do you think is going on? I mean, how is that thing even here?" Cosmo panted.

Harley had barely had a moment to consider it. "All I can think is that my time machine worked in reverse somehow. Rather than sending *me* back in time, it brought *the dinosaur* to me!"

"Perhaps. But in the test run, you were only meant to be travelling back to the day before?"

Cosmo had a point. Harley was sure she'd put the correct date in the settings. Why would it randomly choose to send something from sixty-six million years ago? And the fact it happened to be *her* dinosaur was way too much of a coincidence. "I know. It doesn't make sense." She could feel the answer somewhere just out of reach.

As they hit the main track back to Cogworks, breathless but still sprinting, pupils were starting to make their way to school. The pair hurried past Rufus and Henry, who were chatting intently.

"I tell you, Henry, I saw something flash past my bedroom window just before I left for school. It was giant!"

"Nice one, Rufus. I almost believed you for a second."

Harley and Cosmo exchanged a glance and kept hurrying past.

A couple of pupils from the year above were walking to school ahead, and one was saying: "I know seismic activity when I see it!"

The other responded, "It was definitely an earthquake."

But as Harley and Cosmo reached Cogworks, they saw that the professors were all out by the gate, and Professor Fretshaw was trying to calm down a woman in a large purple dress and crown.

"Hey, that's the woman from the fancy-dress party!" exclaimed Harley, frowning.

Cosmo shrugged. "And what's everyone doing outside?"

"I demand to be let in to my castle!" said the regal woman.

"I keep telling you, this is not your castle; it is my school," said Professor Fretshaw angrily.

"I saw thou flee!" the woman huffed in response. "If it was thine castle, thou would be holding firm. But it matters not, as this castle is in my realm!"

Professor Fretshaw looked to Professor Spark for help. "Really, whichever amateur dramatic society is responsible for this will be held accountable."

"Why is no one going inside?" Harley asked Dolores Dredge, who was sitting beside the gate with her robot snake, watching the curious events with obvious enjoyment.

"It's incredible. Some other actor's taken over the building. He says he's conquered it so it's his, and that queen over there says it's hers."

The front doors of Cogworks opened, and out stepped the soldier that Harley had seen a couple of days ago. "*ego nullam obsidionem superesse!*" he shouted, brandishing his sword again.

"What did he just say?" asked Harley.

"That was Latin," said Cosmo. "I learned some in my old school, thinking it would help with my plant studies. I think he said something about not being taken."

"Whatever it was, it looks like he's not budging," said Dolores. "Fretshaw will be going from angry to boiling fury at any moment!"

"Perhaps it's not a good time to ask for her help with the dinosaur, then," said Cosmo cautiously to Harley.

Dolores turned to look at them. "Dinosaur?"

At that moment, Professor Anning came up to Harley and Cosmo from the drive, looking dazed.

"Professor?" Harley asked. "Are you all right?"

"It was the most peculiar thing," Professor Anning said. "I'm sure I saw a dinosaur heading into the Iron Forest not too long ago. I was certain I'd imagined it … but now this? That man dressed as a Roman soldier?"

Harley felt as though the word "guilty" was flashing across her forehead.

"And earthquakes in Forgetown! When I took this job, I didn't imagine it would be quite so … *interesting*."

Professor Spark joined them. She looked between Harley and Cosmo and lowered her voice. "Harley, is there something you'd like to tell me? Cosmo?"

"I will not be party to a siege on my own school, whether you are a queen or not!" Professor Fretshaw shouted at the queen from the gate.

Things were starting to become achingly clear to Harley: the powerful quakes, the queen, the Roman soldier, the giant bird Fenelda had seen, now the dinosaur. They were all linked to her time-travel machine. It had worked, just not in the way she had intended. She had set off some sort of ripple through time when she had tested it. And with each try a different part of history had been pulled into the present. But how?

"Professors, I, er … I think, that is to say, I, er … *may* have accidentally set off some sort of … time quake."

Suddenly, a call came from Professor Horatio. "There's a giant shelled squid in the Rusty River!"

Then he was knocked off his feet by a running dodo.

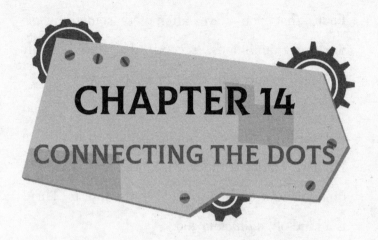

CHAPTER 14
CONNECTING THE DOTS

After Professor Spark and Professor Anning had ushered Harley and Cosmo down the lane a little, away from the commotion at the school, Harley explained what she thought had happened: how her machine had somehow latched on to things from history and brought them into their time, from the soldier to the dodo.

Professor Spark shook her head in disbelief.

"Harley, I must say I'm astounded on many fronts. First, that you have attempted something so dazzlingly ambitious; second, that you actually managed to succeed, albeit in a catastrophic way."

"Ah, there may be a third front," Harley said awkwardly, as Sprocket ran up the lane to join them. He gave Harley a quick wink, and she knew the dinosaur was safely distracted in the forest. "There is a kind of … *dinosaur* too."

"A *kind* of *dinosaur*?" Professor Spark's frown was so deep Harley thought she might fall over.

"I knew I'd seen something!" Professor Anning lit up. "How extraordinary that I got to actually see one after studying them for so long!"

"Hmm, you might not think that when you see it again," said Cosmo. "It's rather fierce-looking."

"And it's in the Iron Forest, for now. What do we do?" asked Harley.

"Have you any idea what connects all the things that have arrived in our time?" asked Professor Anning.

"Well, the dinosaur has six toes, just like in the fossil."

"Really?" Professor Anning's eyes widened.

"And Professor, did you say that was a Roman soldier?" asked Harley. "Because my grandpa Elliot has this lucky Roman coin at home, and the queen…" She thought for a moment, then remembered the framed handkerchief. Then there were the giant ferns and Grandpa Eden's amber, the dodo egg at Cosmo's house, and now a squid-like shell creature in the Rusty River that sounded remarkably like the ammonite creature she'd seen a drawing of in the dinosaur book, and Professor Anning's giant ammonite fossil *was* currently in the school entrance hall right beside Harley's fossil footprint. All artefacts that had been close to where she'd completed her test runs… "Objects!" she exclaimed. Everything that's arrived in our time is related to an artefact that was nearby when I conducted my time-machine tests!"

Professor Anning nodded keenly. "That would

make sense."

"Should I tell Professor Fretshaw yet?" Harley said quietly, knowing it was inevitable.

Professor Spark and Professor Anning looked at each other, and an understanding passed between them.

Professor Spark said, "There's no use worrying Professor Fretshaw and the other teachers. I think we should split up and try to tackle each problem ourselves to prevent the town descending into any further chaos. People will only start to panic if news gets out, and panic creates more problems than it solves."

"Agreed," said Professor Anning.

"Then I'll set tasks for us all. Professor Anning, can you keep an eye on the threat in the Iron Forest?"

With a broad smile, she nodded her head. "Gladly."

"And Cosmo, I seem to remember you took Latin at your old school?"

"I did."

"Then you can set about finding a way of communicating with the Roman soldier so that the pupils and other professors can carry on about their day. I'll placate the queen and tell her we're taking a royal dodo-catching picnic, or some such. That just leaves the river creature, and the rather large matter of putting all this right. Harley, I take it your grandpas are aware of the situation?"

She wriggled awkwardly in her boots. She'd hardly spoken to them lately, what with all her focus being on the time-travel machine. "They may suspect something," she said.

"Then I want you to send a message home and ask them to check on the creature in the Rusty River and make sure it doesn't go further downstream."

"Grandpa Elliot will be at work, but Grandpa Eden will be at home dealing with an … ancient plant pruning situation, so he might be busy." Harley reddened, realizing she hadn't even brought up the amber.

"I see. Any other situations we should know about?"

Harley shook her head.

"Then perhaps I'll just let Professor Horatio in on our situation and he can contact your grandpa Eden and they can tackle the river together. That just leaves you with the rather important task of finding a way to reverse your machine."

"Me? On my own?"

"Harley, you made the machine. I'm certain you can find a way."

Professor Spark seemed so confident that Harley didn't object further. So, with that, everyone set about their tasks. Cosmo gave Harley a sorry shrug as he turned to make his way nervously back to the school to speak to the Roman soldier.

Sprocket whimpered sympathetically.

"I know," Harley said, frowning. "This task is bigger than that dinosaur!"

The truth was, she had managed to make the time-travel machine work more by accident than judgment. How could she reverse something when she wasn't entirely sure how she'd got it working in the first place?

She glanced across to see Fenelda out on the Cogworks lawn. She seemed to be controlling a flock of robot pigeons, getting them to pick up small, wrapped boxes, fly to marked points, drop off the boxes, and then return to where they had picked them up.

Fenelda looked across with a sly smile.

"Having a spot of bother, Harley?" She meaningfully stroked her school uniform lapel where the golden light-bulb badge for Pupil of the Term would sit.

But Harley didn't care about Fenelda's taunts – they were the least of her problems.

Fenelda strode over. "You can't say I didn't warn you to stick with an invention you could handle, something more at your level…"

Of course Fenelda had observed everything that had been going on that morning and put it all together to equal Harley. Harley wished she hadn't told Fenelda about it in the first place.

Harley slumped down to the ground to think. "So I just need to bring all the objects together … and reverse the settings…" she muttered.

"Talking to yourself, Harley?" called Fenelda. "There's a dodo on the loose, if you want some stimulating conversation." She chuckled at her own joke.

Harley's frown deepened. "I just need to send everything back home. That's all I need to do…"

She looked up at Fenelda, and at that moment a glorious idea came to her!

But so did an ice-cold feeling of dread, because her solution required the help of the very last person she wanted to ask.

Fenelda Spiggot.

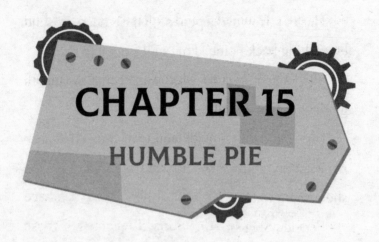

CHAPTER 15

HUMBLE PIE

"Nel."

"Harley."

"About these robot pigeons of yours."

"You mean my expert, precision homing pigeons? The pigeons you said were a 'rubbish idea'?"

"Well, when I said rubbish…"

"The robot pigeons that you thought were somehow inferior to your ridiculously over-ambitious time-travel idea? The robot pigeons with the super-advanced, cutting-edge and expertly crafted add-on homing device?"

"Yes, those blasted pigeons!" Harley snapped, unable to stop herself.

Fenelda smiled smugly and turned away.

It took every ounce of Harley's willpower to cool her boiler. She thought of her grandpa's advice and took a deep breath. "Sorry, I meant, *yes*, those *incredible* pigeons. It's just that I've realized how to solve the rather sticky situation that I'm – I mean, we're all – in." She took another breath, then muttered, "Nel, I need your help."

Fenelda spun round and put a hand to her chest. "*You* want *my* help?" she exclaimed, with fake sweetness.

Harley frowned and nodded.

Fenelda took a step closer. "Oh no, Harley Hitch.

I'm going to need you to say it with much more conviction."

Grandpa Elliot often used the phrase *having to eat humble pie* about situations where someone was forced to give an apology and admit they were wrong. At first, Harley had thought it might be some delicious new dish that Grandpa Elliot had created, but over the years she'd worked out what it meant, of course. But it was only at this moment that she truly *understood* it.

"Fenelda Spiggot, I've known you since we were in nursery together. We were good friends once, and hopefully that counts for something, because yes, I need your help."

Fenelda tilted her head.

"Nel, I need your help, *please.*"

Fenelda gave a satisfied smile. "Then why didn't you just say?"

Cosmo had completed his task well: by the time Harley and Fenelda had made their way to the school, the professors and their classmates were making their way inside, past the Roman soldier – still scowling – at the door.

Professor Spark had presented the queen with tea and cake on the lawn, and she was being waited upon by a row of helpful garden bots.

Harley called over. "Professor Spark, may Fenelda and I use one of the labs to finish my project this morning?"

Professor Spark nodded and winked, so Harley and Fenelda hurried inside to start. Harley had forgotten quite how hard a worker Fenelda was. They used to team up a lot in their early years at school, the years before the cog-flower incident when Fenelda had accused Harley of cheating. They worked quietly and swiftly, opening up the body of the time machine. Harley explained about some of the components and the research she'd carried out, and Fenelda seemed genuinely interested. They decided on the best place for Fenelda's homing mechanism, and after a couple of hours' work, they were ready to go.

Professor Spark came to check on them.

"I think we're set," said Harley. She explained

what they had done and what the plan was.

"Good," said Professor Spark. "The dodo is safely in a pen out the front. The queen seems quite happy now she has an army of servants tending to her. The Roman soldier is on the lawn giving sword-combat lessons to the year sixes, which they are rather enjoying, and thanks to your grandpa Eden, the ammonite is happily bobbing in the school lake, minding its business. We've let Professor Fretshaw continue in her belief that the queen and the soldier are simply part of some dramatic reenactment show from Inventia City, with the aim of enticing pupils into the dramatic arts, and that the dodo is a lifelike automaton which is part of their act. Professor Anning has sent word that the dinosaur is contained, but she would like your help in bringing it back here when the time is right."

"*My* help?" Harley had rather hoped that she

wouldn't have to encounter it again, even though it had been thrilling to see her dinosaur in real life.

"Yes, Professor Anning was very clear it should be you, although Cosmo can accompany you. But we'll need to wait for the pupils and professors to go home. I'll persuade Professor Fretshaw that she should leave early, after such a trying day. Then we'll all meet on the school front lawn and hope that your solution works."

Harley nodded with her fingers tightly crossed for luck.

Harley and Cosmo walked down to the Iron Forest with Sprocket leading the way.

"When I woke up this morning, I never thought that I'd be entering peace talks with a Roman centurion and learning to fight with a sword!" Cosmo said.

"And I never thought I'd be side by side working with Fenelda!"

Cosmo chuckled.

"What?"

"It's just that after all the weird, wonderful and, quite frankly, *life-threatening* things that you've been through today, you choose to highlight that!"

Harley laughed. "I guess that shows just how unusual it was that I worked with her!"

Cosmo's smile dimmed. "Harley, are you nervous about what we'll find in the forest? I mean, trust you to discover the fossil to a gigantic, fierce, silver-clawed monster-saurus!"

"Yeah, why couldn't it have been a cute baby diplodocus?"

"I just hope Professor Anning is all right."

"I'm sure she is. She's probably sedated it or something."

Cosmo stopped suddenly. "But what if it wakes up when we're there?"

"Come on. Stop worrying. You've tamed a Roman soldier today!"

They entered the Iron Forest. After walking for what felt like ages, they eventually walked into a clearing and Harley stopped in disbelief. She could see the dinosaur's feet, but its head was up in the trees ... and there was no Professor Anning.

"Oh no!" Cosmo said, his voice like jelly. "It's eaten her!"

Heart thudding in her chest, Harley couldn't help but think that something awful had happened. She wanted to call out for the professor, but she didn't want to risk alerting the dinosaur to their presence.

"Professor?" she whispered urgently. "Are you hurt? Are you ... alive?"

There was no answer.

"Sprocket, scan the area for human life."

Sprocket's laser eyes penetrated the gloom as he searched. Then a heartbeat pulsed in the screens of his eyes.

She was alive!

"She must be injured," Harley said. "Come on, we have to brave it and help her. Move silently."

They ventured into the clearing, searching the leaves and quietly calling her name.

"Maybe it crushed her with its huge feet?" suggested Cosmo.

Rustling sounded. They both looked up in horror as the dinosaur's head pierced the foliage above, bending down to look straight at them.

CHAPTER 16

GERTIE

"There you are! I was wondering where you'd got to!"

Harley looked up, not only into the huge eyes of the dinosaur, but also, as the dinosaur came towards them through the trees, to see Professor Anning sitting atop the huge beast, legs straddling its back.

"What—? How—?" Harley stuttered.

"I can't tell you what a *marvellous* day I've had with this magnificent animal," the professor said.

"It's not sedated … and it hasn't eaten you?" said Cosmo, perplexed.

Professor Anning slung her leg around and slid down the side of the dinosaur to the ground, then gave it a firm pat on the leg. "Thanks, Gertie."

"Gertie?" asked Harley.

Professor Anning nodded. "It seemed to suit her."

"She's a girl, then?"

"Indeed, and a vegetarian."

Relief made Harley feel as though she was floating.

"It's not going to eat us!" said Cosmo, punching the air.

"Most definitely not," said Professor Anning. "It's amazing what you can find out in such a short time when you have the actual animal in front of you. It's so much easier than working with fragments and fossils. I've discovered that its unusual silver claws evolved especially for an environment such as this forest. It seems rather partial to the leaves of the iron oaks and the cog ferns."

"Wow, really?" Harley asked.

Gertie looked at her with ice-blue eyes and tilted her head. She was sure the dinosaur gave her the hint of a smile.

"Yes, I suspected as much when you told me that she honed in on anything shiny. And that also means that the origins of this unique forest are likely as old as the Jurassic era too!"

"Incredible," said Cosmo.

"Why don't you both give her a stroke?"

Harley reached out her hand and tentatively put her palm to the dinosaur's cheek. It felt rough yet smooth at the same time – tough and a little scaly, but each scale was like velvet. Tingles of excited electricity passed through her.

"Your classmate Fenelda Spiggot let me use one of her precision homing pigeons today, so I've been sending samples and messages to my contacts in Inventia City too. I have exciting news that I wanted to tell you in person."

Harley hoped that the news was that Gertie could stay in the present day … but she knew that wouldn't be fair. Surely Gertie had family back in Jurassic times? She thought of her grandpas, Sprocket and Cosmo, and the thought of being separated from her loved ones by sixty-six million years made her heart twist.

"The Royal Paleontological Society has accepted

that your fossil, Gertie's footprint, shows that she is a six-toed wonder, something unique to her species of dinosaur. It is indeed a new discovery. Congratulations, Harley!"

"That's amazing!"

Cosmo patted her on the shoulder. "Go, Harley – young paleontologist of the year!"

Harley smiled, a warm glow filling her like honey. "So what type of dinosaur is she?" she asked excitedly.

"That's the thing with new discoveries. There is no name yet. I'm going to submit a suggestion. How do you feel about the *Hitchasaurus rex,* no, actually, the *Hitchasaurus regina*? Rex is kingly and your dinosaur is a queen!"

Harley's heart leaped. "Really? That's amazing! I love it!" A whole dinosaur named after her! She couldn't believe it.

They spent some time feeding Gertie cogweed and polishing her claws while Professor Anning told them amazing details about the fossils she'd discovered in her time, the way they were formed, and her favourite prehistoric creatures.

The sun became low in the evening sky.

"We should head back to Cogworks. Do you fancy a ride?" asked Professor Anning.

"In what?" Harley asked. There were no roads through the Iron Forest so transports couldn't come inside.

"Not in, *on*." Professor Anning pointed to the dinosaur.

"Best day ever!" said Harley, as they climbed on to Gertie's back.

Holding on to her violet back spines, they set off.

Back at Cogworks, the grandpas were waiting for Harley.

After their initial shock at seeing the dinosaur, they hurried over and embraced her in a warm hug.

"Harley, what a day you've had!' said Grandpa Elliot.

"It's been one of a kind. And I'm sorry about accidentally covering the house in ferns and vines. I didn't know it was my fault at the time!"

"It's been rather thrilling to see all the different species, to be honest," said Grandpa Eden.

Harley bit her lip awkwardly. "I wanted to surprise you with the time-travel machine. Then things got a little out of hand rather quickly."

Professor Spark approached and said, "Everything is in place. It's time to see if we can finally put this right."

With a nod, Harley put on her time-travel backpack and approached Gertie. "Sorry about taking you out of your own time. But it was very nice to meet you. Tell your family I hope they weren't too worried."

Gertie gave a nod, and Harley patted her side.

"Hold on to your hats, everyone!" Harley braced herself with a long breath in, then put her finger on the button, readying herself for being launched across the grass.

There was a loud *BOOM*, and rather than flying forward, Harley experienced a violent tugging sensation in her belly. Air whooshed backwards as though the world had inhaled, and everything seemed to whirl around her. Then, with a sudden flash of piercing white light, it stopped.

Harley looked around. She was still standing in front of Cogworks. Her grandpas, Cosmo, Fenelda and the professors were still there, looking a bit windswept and ruffled ... but the Roman soldier, the queen, the dodo, the ammonite and Gertie the

Hitchasaurus regina had all vanished back to their own times.

Harley let out a huge sigh of relief.

CHAPTER 17

A PLACE IN TIME

As she took off the time-machine backpack, a strange empty sadness filled Harley. One moment all these things, these amazing historic people and creatures had been close, and now they were gone. Really gone, because in her time, the present, they had died long ago – all that remained were fragments of memory.

Sensing her emotions, her grandpas approached

and took a hand each.

Grandpa Elliot squeezed. "You know, everything has a place in time. Without change there can be no growth. It's moments that matter."

"Grandpa Elliot is right. Moments like this. Not getting stuck in the past, or too hung up on the future. Being together with family and friends. Not taking for granted what you have."

"That's right. I love history, but what I love even more is *now*," Grandpa Elliot said and smiled.

Two weeks later, it was the end of term, and Professor Anning and Professor Spark took centre stage in assembly.

"The time has come for the Pupil of the Term announcement," said Professor Spark.

Harley didn't hold out any hope as she waited for Professor Fretshaw to join them onstage. The head

teacher was unfavourable towards Harley at the best of times, let alone when she'd been letting dinosaurs loose in Forgetown. And there had been some pretty amazing projects, which would make it tough for Professor Fretshaw to decide: Cosmo's Knights of the Slug Realm were finding their way into gardens across Forgetown; Letti's telescopic spoon was causing all sorts of fun in the school canteen; Asma's spring-loaded trainers had made powerball even more fun; and Fenelda's homing robot pigeons had been embraced in Inventia City – not to mention her usual exemplary general scores for the term.

Professor Spark continued: "As this is the school year's final Pupil of the Term, Professor Fretshaw has allowed a deviation from the normal routine. At the request of Professor Anning, she has permitted the other professors to confer and choose a winner.

"After much discussion, we have selected a

student for her exemplary everyday invention, which has had a far-reaching effect, making sending letters and gifts seamless, improving communication across our land and improving efficiency across a wide range of activities in Inventia. But her invention also had an unexpected *larger* impact. Sometimes it's when you help others put things right that the real you starts to shine."

Harley's heart sank. Of course it had to be...

"The winner is ... Fenelda Spiggot!"

Everyone clapped as Fenelda bounced out of her chair and strode to the stage, her grin wide. Harley supposed she couldn't really feel bad about it. Although it pained Harley to admit it, without Fenelda she would still be in a sticky situation.

Then Professor Anning stepped up to the podium. "Things have certainly been interesting since I joined Cogworks. I'm excited to announce that I have agreed to stay another year to teach."

The students all broke into a round of applause and cheers.

Professor Anning smiled and nodded in thanks. "And in the spirit of an unusual term, I would like to announce that the prize of Pupil of the Term will be *shared* this time."

Harley's heart skipped a beat. Shared?

"Our second winner achieved something remarkable by discovering an entirely new species of dinosaur."

The words seemed unreal to Harley. Was Professor Anning really about to say it, or was she imagining what was happening? She could feel the gaze of other pupils begin to turn her way. Cosmo nudged her.

"This pupil also demonstrated that in science, getting things wrong is an important part of the process of discovery. That even failures are successes in science. Our joint winner is … Harley Hitch."

For a moment, all Harley could hear was a rumpus of applause. Pupil of the Term at last! It wasn't quite as she imagined, sharing it with her arch-nemesis. She'd envisaged Fenelda's indignant face watching her as she took the stage, and instead she was already up there, glowing. But, strangely, that didn't feel as bad as she'd thought it would. What was it her grandpas told her once? That jealousy was an ugly colour but trying to make others jealous was an even uglier one.

She walked through the crowd of pupils and took to the stage with a warm shake of the hand from Professors Spark and Anning. They were handed a framed certificate each, and Harley couldn't wait to pin on the golden light-bulb badge.

Professor Spark approached, holding a red velvet

cushion, the shining pin in the centre. "I'm afraid there is only one badge, as it has historic value to the school, so we felt it unfair to try to reproduce it. You'll have to work out how to share it."

Harley and Fenelda both took the edges of the cushion, each feeling the force of each other's tug while smiling for the crowd.

As everyone was dismissed back to their classes to finish the last day of term, Harley and Fenelda remained rooted to the stage, still gripping the cushion.

"We could alternate each week?" suggested Harley.

Fenelda nodded. "F is before H in the alphabet, so I should go first."

"But if we go by second names, H is before S, so *I* should go first."

"Without me, you wouldn't be standing here."

"But I discovered an entire new species and … time travel!"

"But it was such a disaster, no one knows about it!" said Fenelda.

"You've won it before."

"It doesn't make it less special."

Cosmo lingered in front of the stage. "Are you two coming to class?"

They both looked at him. "In a moment."

Then they continued to debate: "But my name was called first."

"Then you should be gracious and let me wear it first."

"Heads or tails?"

"Rock paper scissors?"

Fenelda gave a firm nod.

Harley smiled. She was good at rock paper scissors. She wanted to wear the badge first, but didn't *really* mind; she would get to wear it at some point, and no one could take the title away from her now the term was almost over. Because here she was, standing on the shoulders of giants, which felt pretty good.

"One, two, three."

Harley and Fenelda both made rocks.

"One, two, three."

They both made scissors.

"One, two, three."

They both made paper.

"I'll leave you to it," said Cosmo, shaking his head with a smile and heading off to class.

ACKNOWLEDGEMENTS

My very great ongoing thanks to Scholastic UK, Linas Alsenas, Kate Shaw, George Ermos, Jamie Gregory, Harriet Dunlea, Susila Baybars, Sarah Dutton, and all the booksellers, educators and librarians who have got this series into young hands.

To the reader: I hope, like me, you feel like you have loyal and fun friends in Harley and Cosmo. I've always wanted to put a dinosaur into a story, and I knew that if anyone could make it happen, Harley could!

Vashti Hardy grew up in West Sussex between the hills and the sea, scrambling through brambles and over pebbles. Her middle-grade fantasy novels are now published across the world in several languages. Her debut, *Brightstorm*, was shortlisted for the Waterstones Children's Book Prize and Books Are My Bag Readers Awards, and her second book, *Wildspark*, won the Blue Peter Book Award 'Best Story' in 2020. Vashti now lives in both West Sussex and Lancashire with her husband and three children.

Vashtihardy.com
Twitter @vashti_hardy
Instagram vashtihardyauthor

George Ermos is an illustrator, maker and avid reader from England. He works digitally and loves illustrating all things curious and mysterious. He is always trying to incorporate new artiness from the various world cultures he reads about and explores.

Twitter @georgermos

READ MORE OF
HARLEY'S ADVENTURES: